KW-169-995

# In the Shadow of Knucklas Castle

## a tale of Arthur, Guinevere and the Giants

## by Katy Mac

## for Knucklas Castle Community Land Project

### and for Billy, Jemima and Eliza

YouCaxton Publications
Oxford & Shrewsbury

Copyright © Katy Mac 2017
Copyright illustrations © Katy Mac 2017

The Author asserts the moral right to
be identified as the author of this work.

ISBN 978-1-911175-61-2
Printed and bound in Great Britain.
Published by YouCaxton Publications 2017

All rights reserved. No part of this publication may be reproduced,
stored in a retrieval system, or transmitted in any form or by
any means, electronic, mechanical, photocopying, recording
or otherwise, without the prior permission of the author.

This book is sold subject to the condition that it shall not, by way of
trade or otherwise, be lent, resold, hired out or otherwise circulated
without the author's prior consent in any form of binding or cover
other than that in which it is published and without a similar condition
including this condition being imposed on the subsequent purchaser.

YouCaxton Publications
enquiries@youcaxton.co.uk

## With thanks to:

Wendy and John Davies and Linda Fone for numerous entertaining stories and local details, and Wendy and the art group for so many ideas about the paintings.

Mick Greenway for giving my draft so much thought and all his help knocking it into shape.

Carwen Maggs for stepping in so willingly to explain the Welsh pronunciations – see opposite.

Jamie Ritchie who took the photographs, for his critical eye, for help in all sorts of ways, and above all his tolerance.

Kevin Jones for so much practical help.

Bob Fowke from YouCaxton publishers for his very helpful, expert advice.

To all others who have helped and encouraged in different ways, including the children who let me try out the story on them and their helpful remarks.

Finally to everyone who might buy this book and support the Knucklas Castle Community Land Project.

*Katy Mac*

## Notes on pronunciation for some of the names in the story.

| Welsh Name | Pronunciation |
|---|---|
| Gawr | Gowr - the 'ow' is as in 'how' |
| Brycheiniog | Bricheyene-og – the 'ch' as in 'loch' or 'Bach' |
| Gwenhwyfar | Goowen-hooeevar |
| Bronn Wrgan | Bron Oorgan |
| Cernyw | Kern-ee-you |
| Tyfed-yr-iad | Tuved ur eyed |
| Afon Tefeidiad | Avon Teveyedeead |
| Cornbwch Gawr | Kornbooch Gowr - the 'ch' as in 'Loch' |
| Cnwclas | Cnooclas – the 'C' as in 'cat' |
| Morgannwg | Morgan-oog |

The letter 'r' is always rolled.

KNUCKLAS CASTLE

Castell Kayr

ARTHUR

To Snowdonia
Home of Giant Rhitta

Beguildy

Llanfair Waterdine

Monaughty Poeth

The Stone

Forest of Knucklas

Bloody Field

Knucklas Castle

Heyope

To Brycheiniog and Morgannwg

Radnor Forest

Forest of Blethuagh

N
W        E
S

This is a special hill.

It's in a little Welsh village called Knucklas, or Cnwclas in Welsh, which means 'green mound', and you can see it is a green mound – a large one! Those strange lumps hide all that remains of an ancient castle. In the valley the River Teme winds its way, sometimes gently, sometimes rushing, towards the sea.

If the hill could only talk what stories it could tell. Perhaps it could tell us about the melting of the glaciers. Perhaps it could even tell us about the dinosaurs, what colours they were and the noises they made. I expect it could tell us about the first people who settled near the hill and all the adventures they had. Those days have faded into the mists leaving fragments of history mingled with old legends and mysterious tales.

*A special hill*

This tale is set hundreds of years ago, when the rugged hills and mountains of Wales were covered in forests and giants lurked in caves and valleys. One of the giants was named Gogfran Gawr. Some say he lived in Brycheiniog, deep in the Black Mountains where he was king. Some say he really lived at Knucklas Castle. Sadly I cannot tell you which for certain.

I cannot even tell you if Gogfran was fierce and scary or if he was just a big friendly giant like the BFG. Nor can I tell you what he looked like. He might have been as big as a house. He might have had mean piercing eyes and enormous teeth.

*He might have had mean piercing eyes and enormous teeth*

Or perhaps he looked completely different
– like in this cave painting?

Maybe he was just like everyone else – except
rather large. I like to think so, but, whatever he
looked like, he had a lovely daughter. She was called
Gwenhwyfar. The English call her Guinevere.

You might already know that this was the name of King
Arthur's wife. In this story Arthur had three wives and
would you believe it, each one was called Guinevere.

Arthur's first wife was kidnapped by his nephew, the spiteful Mordred. She tried to escape, but was bitten by a snake as she fled, and, sadly, died. The second had a wicked twin sister who was very jealous. This sister got rid of the real Guinevere, and pretended to be her. She looked so like his wife that Arthur didn't notice. I think she would have got away with it altogether if she hadn't finally felt so guilty that she confessed. I'm afraid that was the end of her.

Arthur, sad and lonely, began his search for another wife.

Guinevere, the daughter of Gogfran, had two brothers whom she loved dearly. They had been taken prisoner by the giants of Bronn Wrgan, a land on the borders of Shropshire on the other side of the River Teme. Poor Guinevere was overwhelmed with grief.

*They had been taken prisoner by the giants of Bronn Wrgan*

But there was no point crying. She needed urgent help but
who would dare face these giants and free her brothers?
She was in despair. Why, even her own father, himself
a giant, was not brave enough to confront them.

Then… she remembered Arthur. Arthur, the man who had
slain the red-eyed giant of Cernyw. Arthur who had tricked and
defeated the three giantesses of Morgannwg, and Arthur, the
man who had sliced in two the greatest giant of all, Giant Rhitta.

He was certainly the one person alive with the skill
and courage to take on such a perilous task.

Guinevere set off at once to find Arthur.

*Guinevere set off at once to find Arthur*

In those days there were no maps – not even like the one at the beginning of this book. Wales had few roads. The ancient tracks for driving cattle were rough and sometimes disappeared altogether leaving only the sun and stars to guide the way. I have already told you about the giants, but there were dragons, wolves and other strange, fierce creatures which stalked the forests. The journey was long, hard and fraught with danger.

Tired and weary, at last she found Arthur and pleaded with him to come. Surely even Arthur, that great warrior, must have been a little frightened. This wasn't just one giant but a whole *land* of giants. Perhaps it was Guinevere's brave, determined spirit that persuaded him, or perhaps it was her gentle voice and beseeching eyes, or perhaps Arthur, though scared, could not resist the challenge. I expect it was a mixture of all these things but, before the day ended, Arthur had set off to fight the giants.

*There were dragons, wolves and other strange fierce creatures which stalked the forests*

He knew it would not be easy. One man alone could hardly kill all of these giants. He would need all his wits about him.

Arthur decided he should start by killing the biggest and most powerful giant. I do not know whether he won in a straight fight or through trickery, but, against all the odds, Arthur was victorious. Somehow he managed to kill the biggest giant as well as several of the others and he freed Guinevere's brothers.

Maybe the rest ran away in fear or perhaps he overpowered them with his powerful sword, Excalibur – the sword which the Lady of the Lake had given him as protection from danger.

*He killed the biggest giant as well as several others and he freed Guinevere's brothers*

As you would expect, they were all anxious to leave Bronn Wrgan, land of giants, as quickly as possible. But they needed to cross the River Teme, and when they came to its banks the water was rushing wildly and it was so wide and deep that none could cross. Luckily Arthur had an idea. He cut off the giant's head and threw it into the river so it could be used as a stepping stone.

As Arthur crossed the river he called out 'tyfed-yr-iad' meaning 'let the head turn to stone in the water', and, would you believe it, that's just what it did. It turned to stone. This is how the River Teme got its Welsh name, Afon Tefeidiad.

*'let the head turn to stone in the water'*

Imagine how happy Arthur and Guinevere were! The giants had been defeated and her brothers were free. What is more Arthur and Guinevere were by now very much in love.

They rode on to Knucklas Castle filled with joy, and before they arrived they had decided to marry.

The wedding took place in the castle. There must have been great celebrations with feasting and merry-making throughout the land, and I think they lived happily ever after.

*The wedding took place in the castle*

Now you may wonder if the giant's head really did turn into a stone. Perhaps it did.  Perhaps it is the great stone that can be seen in a field close to the river near Beguildy. Look closely. You can see the giant's face – not a pretty sight!

But wait.

This stone is not in the river so can it really be the same giant's head that Arthur threw into the Teme?

Perhaps it was in the river and the river changed its course? Maybe. Rivers do this over time.

Or could this be what really happened…?

*Look closely. You can see the giant's face – not a pretty sight*

Further down the River Teme beyond Knucklas was the home of the giant, Cornbwch Gawr. He liked to sit on the great rock called Craig-y-Don which overlooks the river. Maybe it was here that Arthur crossed the Teme and threw the giant's head into the water? Maybe it was here that the giant's head turned to stone?

It is said that, one day, the Devil came and seated himself on the giant's chair at Craig-y-Don. Seeing the stone in the water he pulled it out and hurled it towards the little village of Heyope. Perhaps he was aiming at the castle. Luckily he was a rotten shot. He missed both castle and village and the stone landed harmlessly several miles beyond. This could explain how the stone came to be in the field near Beguildy where it lies to this day.

*Seeing the stone in the water he pulled it out and hurled it towards the little village of Heyope*

Of course Arthur couldn't really turn giants' heads to stone, and there wasn't really a devil seated on Craig-y-Don throwing boulders. And, of course, we know there weren't really even any giants…

except…….

Many years ago, in an ancient tomb in the shadow of the castle, five enormous skeletons were found. Might these have been the bones of those fearsome giants?

Sadly, this is yet another thing I cannot tell you,

but…

I'm sure that old castle hill knows.

## About the Story

This story is largely based on the tale recorded by the C16th Welsh scholar Siôn Dafydd Rhys, compiled from older, now lost, manuscripts. I have relied on the Welsh Classical Dictionary and translations by the Celtic Literature Collective as well as different versions of Arthurian legends and local folklore.

**Knucklas or Cnwclas** is a small village in the Welsh Marches, It looks across to Offa's Dyke - the fortification built in the eighth century that was once the border.

**Castell Cnwclas** is the Welsh for Knucklas Castle.

**Gawr** means 'giant' in Welsh

**Gogfran Gawr** appears in early Welsh legends, sometimes as Gogyrfan Gawr, sometimes Ogfran Gawr and there are other variants of his name.

**Did Knucklas Castle belong to Gogfran Gawr, or to King Arthur?**
Knucklas Castle is thought to be 'Kayr Ogheruen', part of Abbey Cwmhir estates, Ogheruen being another variant of Gogfran. However the Welsh Classical Dictionary states that Gogfran lived in Brycheiniog (Brecknockshire). Richard of Worcester, a historian writing in the C15th says that Knucklas Castle was founded by King Arthur. Siôn Dafydd Rhys seems to agree, saying of Knucklas Castle 'And there was Arthur of old, and from there he married Gwenhwyfar'. Later the C17th scholar Edward Lhuyd tells us the castle had been known as Castell Pendragon'. Uther Pendragon was the name of Arthur's father.

**The Stone** This is on private land: Map ref SO201791

*CRAIG-Y-DON*

**Giant Skeletons** According to the late C19th historian, Jonathan Williams in 'The History of Radnorshire', five very large skeletons were found in a pre-Christian burial chamber at Monaughty Poeth, near the castle. The mound was excavated in the early 1800's and the find confirmed in a government report. It is not known how large the skeletons were, or what happened to the bones.

**Gold Torcs and other ancient remains**
Less than a mile from the castle three Bronze Age gold torcs were found - now in Cardiff Museum. They clearly pre-date King Arthur, who, if he existed, is thought to be C5th or C6th. A silver sword handle from a later date was discovered in the nearby brook. One theory is that this was a site of sacred springs and the treasures were thrown into the water as offerings to the gods. In addition Roman remains were discovered in Knucklas.

**Craig-y-Don** Map ref SO263737. There is a public footpath to this. It is very eerie and certainly a fitting home for a giant. Cornbwch Gawr was said to have lived there but little else seems to be known about him. Perhaps the original story was that it was he, rather than the Devil who threw the stone? Local people say that the devil shouted 'hey-op' as he hurled it, and so the village of Heyope got its name. Some speak of a secret tunnel under the Teme from Craig-y-Don to Skyborry – there are stories of it being used as a hideout or even as an escape route for monks from the Priory near Monaughty Poeth - but that's another story!

## About the Knucklas Castle Community Land Project

**Knucklas Castle Hill** is a scheduled ancient monument overlooking Knucklas village. It is of great natural beauty and a haven for wildlife. The view from the top is stunning. You can see for miles in all directions. Hardly surprising then that they chose to build a castle here.

A few years ago the castle hill, with its surrounding woodland and fields, came up for sale. The buyers wanted it to be used as a community resource and leased the land to the newly formed Knucklas Castle Community Land Project. Its members began by improving access, repairing and making new footpaths, providing a map and setting up benches for people to rest and enjoy the view while making the steep climb to the top.

Wildlife surveys were undertaken, bat and bird boxes put up in the woods.

On the grassy summit, a grazing cycle was established to encourage wild flowers, which flower in abundance.

In the fields below a large community orchard has been planted and allotments established, with the aim of creating a more sustainable local community. There are hens, beehives and plenty of organic vegetables. One allotment is set aside for the sole use of local children, to enable them to learn how things grow and the importance of looking after the environment.

Several community events are held each year, including a Wassail, an Allotment Day and an Apple Day. From the outset there has been a strong emphasis on the arts, with sculpture trails, painting, poetry and music being regular features.

The history of the site is of considerable interest. The 'Bloody Field' by the mound is thought to be where the Battle of Beguildy - of uncertain date and between uncertain combatants - was fought. The stone castle was built in the early 13th century, by order of Ralph de Mortimer, then head of the powerful Marcher family. This was largely destroyed in 1262 by an army led by Llywelyn ap Gruffydd ("Prince Llywelyn"). It was little used thereafter and further destroyed by Owain Glyndwr in 1402. Most of the stone is now gone, much into the fine Victorian viaduct that runs through the village. On the insistence of the then owner of the castle, castellated turrets and battlements were added to the viaduct in return for the castle's stone.

Aerial photographs show outlines of what is probably an earlier Iron Age fort and the Project has ambitions for full archaeological investigations. As the story suggests, the hill surely holds many secrets under the ground.

The Project is actively engaged in raising funds to purchase the land outright. Members of the public are encouraged to buy shares in the Project and help to secure its long term future as a community resource. Donations are welcome, as are volunteers who can become involved in all sorts of ways.

All proceeds from this book will go to the Knucklas Castle Community Land Project (Registered IPS No.30635R)

www.knucklascastle.org.uk

*Castle hill summit with the 'Dragon's Tooth' by Rolf Hook*